Baa, baa, black sheep,
  Have you any wool?
    Yes sir, yes sir,
Three bags full;
One for the master,
And one for the dame,
And one for the little boy
Who lives down the lane.

B.B. BLACKSHEEP AND COMPANY

A COLLECTION OF FAVORITE NURSERY RHYMES ILLUSTRATED BY

NICK BUTTERWORTH

Publishers · GROSSET & DUNLAP · New York

ISBN: 0-448-16577-5. LOC: 82-80874. First published 1981 by Macdonald and Company Limited.
Text copyright © 1981 Macdonald Publishers Ltd. Illustrations copyright © 1981 Nick Butterworth. First U.S. Printing 1982.

There was an old woman
  Who lived in a shoe,
  She had so many children
She didn't know what to do;
She gave them some broth
Without any bread;
Then whipped them all soundly
And put them to bed.

There was a crooked man,
  And he walked a crooked mile,
He found a crooked sixpence
Against a crooked stile;
He bought a crooked cat,
Which caught a crooked mouse,
And they all lived together
In a little crooked house.

Mary, Mary, quite contrary,
  How does your garden grow?
With silver bells and cockle shells,
And pretty maids all in a row.

Jack and Jill went up the hill
To fetch a pail of water;
Jack fell down and broke his crown,
And Jill came tumbling after.

Up Jack got, and home did trot,
As fast as he could caper,
He went to bed to mend his head
With vinegar and brown paper.

Simple Simon met a pieman,
Going to a fair;
Said Simple Simon to the pieman,
Let me taste your ware.

Said the pieman to Simple Simon
Show me first your penny;
Said Simple Simon to the pieman,
Sir, I have not any.

Three blind mice, three blind mice,
See how they run! See how they run!
They all ran after the farmer's wife,
Who cut off their tails with a carving knife,
Did ever you see such a thing in your life
As three blind mice?

Old King Cole was a merry old soul,
And a merry old soul was he;
He called for his pipe, and he called
for his bowl,
And he called for his fiddlers three.

Every fiddler had a fine fiddle,
And a very fine fiddle had he:
Twee, tweedle dee, tweedle dee, went
the fiddlers.
Oh, there's none so rare as can compare
With King Cole and his fiddlers three!

Doctor Foster
    Went to Gloucester
  In a shower of rain;
He stepped in a puddle,
Right up to his middle,
And never went there again.

Hickety, pickety, my black hen,
    She lays eggs for gentlemen;
Gentlemen come every day
To see what my black hen doth lay.
Sometimes nine and sometimes ten,
Hickety, pickety, my black hen.

Rub-a-dub-dub,
    Three men in a tub,
And who do you think they be?
The butcher, the baker,
The candlestick maker,
They all fell out of a rotten potato,
Turn 'em out knaves all three!

Wee Willie Winkie
Runs through the town,
Upstairs and downstairs
In his nightgown,
Rapping at the window,
Crying through the lock,
Are the children in their beds?
It's past eight o'clock!

Goosey, goosey, gander,
Whither shall I wander?
Upstairs and downstairs,
And in my lady's chamber.
There I met an old man
Who would not say his prayers.
I took him by the left leg
And threw him down the stairs.

To bed, to bed, says Sleepy Head,
Tarry a while, says Slow;
Put on the pan, says Greedy Nan,
Let's sup before we go!

Polly put the kettle on,
Polly put the kettle on,
Polly put the kettle on,
We'll all have tea.

Sukey take it off again,
Sukey take it off again,
Sukey take it off again,
They've all gone away.

Pat-a-cake, pat-a-cake, baker's man,
    Bake me a cake as fast as you can;
Pat it and prick it, and mark it with B,
Put it in the oven for baby and me.

Little Jack Horner
    Sat in the corner,
Eating his Christmas pie;
He put in his thumb,
And pulled out a plum,
And said, What a good boy am I!

Incey Wincey spider,
  Climbed the water spout;
  Down came the rain and
  Washed the spider out.
Out came the sun and
Dried up all the rain;
Incey Wincey spider,
Climbed up the spout again.

Barber, barber, shave a pig,
  How many hairs to make a wig?
Four and twenty, that's enough;
Give the barber a pinch of snuff.

Little Miss Muffet
  Sat on a tuffet,
Eating her curds and whey;
There came a big spider,
Who sat down beside her
And frightened Miss Muffet away.

The north wind doth blow,
   And we shall have snow,
And what will poor robin do then?
Poor thing.

He'll sit in the barn
And keep himself warm,
And hide his head under his wing.
Poor thing.

Little Boy Blue, come blow your horn,
   The sheep's in the meadow, the cow's
      in the corn;
But where's the boy who looks after
      the sheep?
He's under the haystack, fast asleep.
Will you wake him? No, not I,
For if I do, he's sure to cry.

Pussycat, pussycat,
    Where have you been?
I've been to London
To look at the Queen.

Pussycat, pussycat,
What did you there?
I frightened a little mouse
Under her chair.

The Queen of Hearts,
    She made some tarts,
All on a summer's day.
The Knave of Hearts,
He stole those tarts,
And took them clean away.

The King of Hearts
Called for the tarts,
And beat the Knave full sore;
The Knave of Hearts
Brought back the tarts,
And vowed he'd steal no more.

Jack be nimble,
    Jack be quick,
Jack jump over
The candlestick.

Hot cross buns!
    Hot cross buns!
One a penny, two a penny,
Hot cross buns!
If you have no daughters,
Give them to your sons,
One a penny, two a penny,
Hot cross buns!

Ring a ring o' roses,
    A pocket full of posies,
Atishoo! Atishoo!
We all fall down.

Mary had a little lamb,
Its fleece was white as snow;
And everywhere that Mary went
The lamb was sure to go.

It followed her to school one day,
That was against the rule;
It made the children laugh and play
To see a lamb at school.

And so the teacher turned it out,
But still it lingered near,
And waited patiently about
Till Mary did appear.

And then it ran to her and laid
Its head upon her arm,
As if it said, I'm not afraid,
You'll keep me from all harm.

Why does the lamb love Mary so?
The eager children cry;
Why, Mary loves the lamb, you know,
The teacher did reply.

Hey diddle diddle,
    The cat and the fiddle,
    The cow jumped over the moon;
The little dog laughed
To see such sport,
And the dish ran away with the spoon.

Old Mother Hubbard
    Went to the cupboard,
To fetch her poor dog a bone;
But when she got there
The cupboard was bare,
And so the poor dog had none.

Cock-a-doodle doo!
    My dame has lost her shoe,
My master's lost his fiddling stick
And doesn't know what to do.

Jack Sprat could eat no fat,
His wife could eat no lean,
And so between them both, you see,
They licked the platter clean.

One, two, three, four, five,
Once I caught a fish alive,
Six, seven, eight, nine, ten,
Then I let it go again.
Why did you let it go?
Because it bit my finger so.
Which finger did it bite?
This little finger on the right.

Bye baby bunting,
Daddy's gone a-hunting.
Gone to fetch a rabbit skin,
To wrap the baby bunting in.

ittle Bo-Peep has lost her sheep,
And can't tell where to find them;
Leave them alone, and they'll
come home,
Bringing their tails behind them.

Little Bo-Peep fell fast asleep,
And dreamt she heard them bleating;
But when she awoke, she found it a joke,
For they were still all fleeting.

Then up she took her little crook,
Determined for to find them;
She found them indeed, but it made
her heart bleed,
For they'd left their tails behind them.

It happened one day, as Bo-Peep did stray
Into a meadow hard by,
There she espied their tails side by side,
All hung on a tree to dry.

She heaved a sigh, and wiped her eye,
And over the hillocks went rambling,
And tried what she could, as a
shepherdess should,
To tack again each to its lambkin.

Early to bed,
Early to rise,
Makes a man healthy,
Wealthy and wise.

Sing a song of sixpence,
A pocket full of rye;
Four and twenty blackbirds,
Baked in a pie!
When the pie was opened,
The birds began to sing;
Now wasn't that a dainty dish
To set before the king?

The king was in his counting house,
Counting out his money;
The queen was in the parlor,
Eating bread and honey.
The maid was in the garden,
Hanging out the clothes;
When down came a blackbird,
And pecked off her nose.

Humpty Dumpty sat on a wall,
Humpty Dumpty had a great fall.
All the king's horses, and all the king's men,
Couldn't put Humpty together again.

O the grand old Duke of York.
He had ten thousand men;
He marched them up to the top of the hill,
And he marched them down again.
And when they were up, they were up,
And when they were down, they were down,
And when they were only halfway up,
They were neither up nor down.

Ride a cock-horse to Banbury Cross,
To see a fine lady upon a white horse;
With rings on her fingers and bells on
   her toes,
She shall have music wherever she goes.

See-saw, Margery Daw,
  Jacky shall have a new master;
He shall have but a penny a day,
Because he can't work any faster.

Hush-a-bye, baby, on the tree top,
  When the wind blows the cradle will rock,
When the bough breaks the cradle will fall,
Down will come baby, cradle and all.

Tom, Tom, the piper's son,
  Stole a pig, and away he run.
The pig was eat, and Tom was beat,
And Tom went roaring down the street.

Georgie Porgie, pudding and pie,
  Kissed the girls and made them cry;
When the boys came out to play,
Georgie Porgie ran away.

To market, to market,
   To buy a fat pig;
Home again, home again,
Jiggety jig.

To market, to market,
To buy a fat hog;
Home again, home again,
Joggety jog.

Ding, dong, bell,
   Pussy's in the well.
Who put her in?
Little Johnny Green.
Who pulled her out?
Little Tommy Stout.
What a naughty boy was that,
To try to drown poor pussycat,
Who never did him any harm,
And killed all the mice
In his father's barn.

Hickory, dickory, dock,
The mouse ran up the clock.
The clock struck one,
The mouse ran down,
Hickory, dickory, dock.

A diller, a dollar,
A ten o'clock scholar,
What makes you come so soon?
You used to come at ten o'clock,
But now you come at noon.

Yankee Doodle came to town,
Riding on a pony;
He stuck a feather in his cap
And called it macaroni.

Twinkle, twinkle, little star,
    How I wonder what you are!
Up above the world so high,
Like a diamond in the sky.

When the blazing sun is gone,
When he nothing shines upon,
Then you show your little light,
Twinkle, twinkle, all the night.

Then the traveler in the dark,
Thanks you for your tiny spark,
He could not tell which way to go,
If you did not twinkle so.

In the dark blue sky you keep,
And often through my curtains peep,
For you never shut your eye,
Till the sun is in the sky.

As your bright and tiny spark,
Lights the traveler in the dark,
Though I know not what you are,
Twinkle, twinkle, little star.